FROG
GOES TO DINNER

by Mercer Mayer

DIAL BOOKS FOR YOUNG READERS
New York

For Tereska and Bob

Published by Dial Books for Young Readers
A division of E. P. Dutton | A division of New American Library
2 Park Avenue, New York, New York 10016
Copyright © 1974 by Mercer Mayer. All rights reserved.
Library of Congress Catalog Card Number: 74-2881
Printed in Hong Kong by South China Printing Co.
COBE
8 10 12 14 15 13 11 9